Here's what kids have to say about reading Magic Tree House® books and Magic Tree House® Merlin Missions:

Thank you for writing these great books! I have learned a great deal of information about history and the world around me.—Rosanna

Your series, the Magic Tree House, was really influential on my late childhood years. [Jack and Annie] taught me courage through their rigorous adventures and profound friendship, and how they stuck it out through thick and thin, from start to finish.—Joe

Your description is fantastic! The words pop out . . . oh, man . . . [the Magic Tree House series] is really exciting!—Christina

I like the Magic Tree House series. I stay up all night reading them. Even on school nights!—Peter

I think I've read about twenty-five of your Magic Tree House books! I'm reading every Magic Tree House book I can get my hands on!—Jack

Never stop writing, and if you can't think about anything to write about, don't worry, use some of my ideas!!—Kevin

Parents, teachers, and librarians love Magic Tree House® books, too!

[Magic Tree House] comes up quite a bit at parent/ teacher conferences.... The parents are amazed at how much more reading is being done at home because of your books. I am very pleased to know such fun and interesting reading exists for students.... Your books have also made students want to learn more about the places Jack and Annie visit. What wonderful starters for some research projects!—Kris L.

As a librarian, I have seen many happy young readers coming into the library to check out the next Magic Tree House book in the series. I have assisted young library patrons with finding nonfiction materials related to the Magic Tree House book they have read. ... The message you are sending to children is invaluable: siblings can be friends; boys and girls can hang out together....—Lynne H.

[My daughter] had a slow start reading, but somehow with your Magic Tree House series, she has been inspired and motivated to read. It is with such urgency that she tracks down your books. She often blurts out various facts and lines followed by "I read that in my Magic Tree House book."—Jenny E.

[My students] seize every opportunity they can to reread a Magic Tree House book or look at all the wonderful illustrations. Jack and Annie have opened a door to a world of literacy that I know will continue throughout the lives of my students.—Deborah H.

[My son] carries his Magic Tree House books everywhere he goes. He just can't put the book he is reading down until he finishes it. . . . He is doing better in school overall since he has made reading a daily thing. He even has a bet going with his aunt that if he continues doing well in school, she will continue to buy him the next book in the Magic Tree House series.—Rosalie R.

MAGIC TREE HOUSE® #38
A MERLIN MISSION

Monday
with a
Mad Genius

by Mary Pope Osborne

illustrated by Sal Murdocca

SCHOLASTIC INC.
New York Toronto London Auckland
Sydney Mexico City New Delhi Hong Kong

ISBN 978-0-545-29377-8

Text copyright © 2007 by Mary Pope Osborne.
Illustrations copyright © 2007 by Sal Murdocca.
Temporary tattoo illustrations copyright © 2009 by Sal Murdocca.
All rights reserved. Published by Scholastic Inc., 557 Broadway, New York, NY 10012, by arrangement with Random House Children's Books, a division of Random House, Inc.
Magic Tree House is a registered trademark of Mary Pope Osborne; used under license.
SCHOLASTIC and associated logos are trademarks and/or registered trademarks of Scholastic Inc.

12 11 10 9 8 7 6 5 4 3 2 1   10 11 12 13 14 15/0

Printed in the U.S.A.   40

This edition first printing, September 2010

For James Quinn Courts

Dear Reader,

During spring vacation when I was in kinder-garten, my brothers and I decided we'd try to fly like birds. We knew that people couldn't fly, but that didn't stop us. We were excited by the thought that we'd be the first to do so. For our launch pad, we chose the playground near our house. We tried swinging and then leaping into the air, flapping our arms wildly. Of course, we kept falling to the ground. Next we climbed to the top of the slide and took turns jumping off, again flapping as hard as we could—only to drop again and again to the sand beneath the slide. We were lucky that we didn't get hurt. All morning we tried to fly, until finally we gave up and went home, satisfied that we'd given it our best shot.

The great thing about being a kid, I think, is that your imagination can make life full of won-drous adventures. Leonardo da Vinci, one of the world's greatest geniuses, was a lot like a kid who never completely grew up. Even when he was working, he seemed to be playing, always looking at the world and asking, "I wonder what would happen if . . ." He had great enthusiasm for experimenting with different ways of doing things and for exploring new ideas—including trying to fly! I hope that when you meet Leonardo in this new Merlin Mission, you will feel that you've made an amazing new friend.

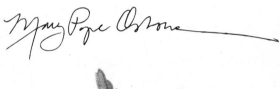

CONTENTS

"I wish to work miracles."
—from the notebooks of
Leonardo da Vinci

Prologue

One summer day in Frog Creek, Pennsylvania, a mysterious tree house appeared in the woods. A brother and sister named Jack and Annie soon learned that the tree house was magic—it could take them to any time and any place in history! And no time at all would pass in Frog Creek while they were gone.

Jack and Annie also learned that the tree house belonged to Morgan le Fay, a magical librarian from the legendary realm of Camelot. After they went on many adventures for Morgan, Merlin the magician began sending Jack and Annie on "Merlin Missions" in the tree house. With help from two young sorcerers named Teddy and Kathleen, Jack and Annie visited four *mythical* places and found valuable objects to help save Camelot.

On their next four Merlin Missions, Jack and Annie once again traveled to real times and real places in history. After proving to Merlin that they knew how to use magic wisely, he entrusted them with the Wand of Dianthus. With the help of the wand, Jack and Annie would now be able to make their *own* magic.

On their most recent adventure, Teddy and Kathleen told Jack and Annie that Merlin was very unhappy and not well and that Morgan wanted them to search for four of the secrets of happiness to share with Merlin.

Now Jack and Annie are waiting for the tree house to return and take them on their second mission to help Merlin. . . .

CHAPTER ONE

Old Friends

Jack poured milk over his cereal. His stomach felt fluttery. It was Monday—the first day of a new school year.

Jack always felt nervous on the first day. What would his new teacher be like? Would his desk be close to a window? Would friends from last year be in his class again this year?

"Annie, hurry!" Jack's mom called upstairs. "It's fifteen minutes till eight. School starts in half an hour."

Jack's dad walked into the kitchen. "Are you

sure you and Annie don't want me to drive you?" he asked.

"No thanks, we don't mind walking," said Jack. Their school was only three blocks away.

"Annie, *hurry*!" their mom called again. "You're going to be late!"

The back door banged open. Annie rushed into the kitchen. She was out of breath.

"Oh, I thought you were upstairs," their mom said with surprise. "You were outside?"

"Yes!" said Annie, panting. "Just taking a quick walk." She looked at Jack. Her eyes sparkled. "Hurry, Jack. We really should go *now*!"

"Okay, I'm coming!" said Jack. He leapt up from the table. He could tell Annie wasn't talking about school. *The tree house must be back! Finally!*

Jack grabbed his backpack. Annie held the door open for him.

"No breakfast?" their mom asked.

"Too nervous to eat now, Mom," said Jack.

"Me too," said Annie. "Bye, Mom! Bye, Dad!"

"Have fun," their mom said.

"Learn a lot," said their dad.

"Don't worry, we will!" said Annie.

Jack and Annie slipped out the door and walked quickly across their yard.

"It's back!" said Annie.

"I figured it was!" said Jack.

"Morgan must want us to look for another secret of happiness to help Merlin," said Annie.

"Yep!" said Jack. "Let's run!"

Jack and Annie dashed up the sidewalk. They crossed the street and headed into the Frog Creek woods. They ran between the trees, through shadows and light, until they came to the tallest oak.

High in the tree was the magic tree house. The rope ladder was swaying in the chilly morning wind.

"How did you know it was here?" asked Jack, catching his breath.

"I woke up thinking about Teddy and Kathleen," said Annie, "and I had this strange feeling."

"Really?" said Jack. "Teddy! Kathleen!" he shouted up at the tree house.

Two young teenagers looked out the tree house window: a curly-haired boy with freckles and a big grin and a smiling girl with sea-blue eyes and dark wavy hair.

"Jack! Annie!" the girl said.

"Come up! Come up!" said the boy.

Jack and Annie hurried up the rope ladder. When they climbed inside the tree house, they threw their arms around their friends.

"Are we going to look for another secret of happiness?" said Annie. "To help Merlin?"

"Yes, and this time you will travel back to Florence, Italy, five hundred years ago," said Teddy.

"Florence, Italy?" said Jack. "What's there?"

"An amazing person who will help you," said Kathleen.

"Who?" asked Annie. "Is this person magical?"

Teddy grinned. "Some people might say so," he said. He reached into his cloak and pulled out a book. The cover showed a drawing of a man wearing a purple cloak and floppy blue cap. He had a long nose, bright, kind eyes with heavy eyebrows, and a flowing beard. The title said:

"Leonardo da Vinci!" said Jack. "Are you kidding?"

"I've heard of him," said Annie.

"Who hasn't?" said Jack. "He was an incredible genius!"

"This biography of Leonardo will help you on your mission," said Teddy.

"And so will this rhyme from Morgan," said Kathleen. She pulled a small piece of parchment paper from her cloak and gave it to Annie.

Annie read the words on the paper aloud.

To Jack and Annie of Frog Creek:

Though the question is quite simple,
Simple answers might be wrong.
If you want to know the right one,
Help the genius all day long,
Morning, noon, and afternoon,
Till the night bird sings its song.

"So to find the secret of happiness, we need to spend the whole day helping Leonardo da Vinci," said Jack.

"Yes," said Kathleen. Teddy nodded.

"I wish you could come, too," said Annie.

"And help *us*," said Jack.

"Never fear," said Kathleen. "You will have the help of the great genius and the Wand of Dianthus."

"Oh!" Annie said to Jack. "Did you bring our wand?"

"Of course," said Jack. "I always carry it with me for safekeeping." He reached into his backpack and pulled out a gleaming silver wand.

"The Wand of Dianthus," Teddy said in a hushed voice.

The wand looked like the horn of a unicorn. It burned in Jack's hand—with cold or warmth, he couldn't tell which. He carefully put the wand back into his pack.

"Remember the three rules of the wand?" said Kathleen.

"Sure," said Annie. "You can only use it for the good of others. You can only use it after you've tried your hardest. And you can only use it with a command of *five* words."

"Excellent," said Kathleen.

"Thanks," said Annie. "Ready?" she asked Jack.

Jack nodded. "Bye, Teddy. Bye, Kathleen."

"Good-bye," said Teddy.

"And good luck," said Kathleen.

Jack pointed at the cover of the book. "I wish we could go to Leonardo da Vinci!"

In the distance, the school bell started to ring, letting kids know that school would start in ten minutes. But in the Frog Creek woods, the wind started to blow.

The tree house started to spin.

It spun faster and faster.

Then everything was still.

Absolutely still.

CHAPTER TWO

Looking for Leonardo

A different bell was bonging in the distance. Bright early sunlight poured through the tree house window. Teddy and Kathleen were gone.

Jack looked down at his clothes. He was wearing a knee-length tunic and dark tights. Annie wore a long dress with puffy sleeves. Jack's backpack had changed into a cloth bag.

Jack and Annie looked out the window. The tree house had landed in a tall tree in a garden surrounded by green hedges. Beyond the garden was a sea of red-tiled roofs. A huge eight-sided

dome and a stone tower rose high above the red
rooftops.

"Welcome to Florence, Italy," said Annie.

Jack opened their book and read aloud:

In the early 1500s, many artists and craftspeople lived in the city of Florence. The city was filled with silk weavers, potters, and marble workers. Artists made sculptures, paintings, and tapestries.

"Cool," said Annie. "I love art."

Jack read more:

But the most amazing genius of that time did a bit of everything. Leonardo da Vinci was not only a great painter but also an inventor, architect, stage and costume designer, horseman, chef, geologist, and botanist.

"What's a *geologist* and a *botanist*?" said Annie.

"They're scientists," said Jack. "A geologist studies rocks, and a botanist studies plants." He turned the page.

"Come on, we should go," said Annie. "The

tree house probably brought us right to Leonardo. We have to find him before he gets away!"

"Oh, right," said Jack.

Annie started down the ladder. Jack packed up their research book and climbed down after her.

Jack and Annie walked around the tall hedge and came to a busy road that ran along a river. They stared at all the people going by. There were women in long silk dresses, priests in black robes riding donkeys, and soldiers in blue capes riding horses.

"I don't see anyone who looks like the guy on the cover of our book," said Jack.

"Let's ask someone," said Annie. She walked over to a girl selling flowers by the road. "Excuse me. Do you know a person named Leonardo da Vinci?"

"Of course! *Everyone* knows Leonardo!" said the girl. "He was just here! He bought some flowers from me. He said he was going to sketch them later." Her eyes shone with excitement.

"Where did he go?" asked Jack.

"He headed toward the Old Bridge," the girl said. She pointed toward a covered bridge farther down the road.

"Thanks!" said Annie.

Jack and Annie walked quickly along the bank of the river toward the bridge. "You were right," said Jack. "The tree house brought us right to Leonardo. But while we were talking, he kept walking."

"Don't worry," said Annie. "We'll catch up to him."

The covered bridge was supported by three stone arches. It looked like a long house stretching over the river.

As they crossed the bridge, it was hard to look for Leonardo. The light was dim and the walkway inside the bridge was filled with people.

Jack and Annie squeezed through the crowd

to the other side of the bridge. The sunlight was so bright that Jack still couldn't see clearly. He shaded his eyes with his hand. "I still don't see him," he said.

"We can ask again," said Annie. "That girl said *everyone* knows Leonardo!" She headed to a shop near the riverbank. Weavers were hanging colorful fabrics on a line. The red and purple silks waved in the breeze.

"Excuse me!" Annie called. "Have you seen Leonardo da Vinci this morning?"

A toothless old woman smiled. "Oh, yes! Leonardo passed by only a moment ago," she said. "On his way to the bakery, I think." She pointed down a narrow lane. "He goes there every morning."

"Thanks!" said Annie.

Jack and Annie hurried to the bakery. The delicious smell of baking bread filled the air.

"Excuse me, did Leonardo da Vinci come in here?" Jack asked.

"Yes, he just bought his daily loaf of bread," said the baker. "He always goes to the cheese shop next." He pointed across the street.

"Thanks!" said Jack.

Jack and Annie crossed the busy street to the cheese shop. "Is Leonardo da Vinci here?" asked Annie.

"He just left," said the cheese man. He pointed up the street. "He was going to the blacksmith's."

"Oh, brother," said Jack.

"Thanks!" said Annie, and they headed up the street.

"I can't wait to meet him!" said Annie.

"Me too," said Jack. "If we ever catch up to him."

Loud hammering noises were coming from a shop. Jack and Annie looked inside and saw a blacksmith pounding a horseshoe with a huge iron hammer. A fire was roaring in a hearth nearby.

"Excuse me!" Jack shouted.

The burly man stopped pounding.

"Was Leonardo da Vinci just here?" asked Jack.

"Yes, he paid me for his iron pots," the blacksmith said gruffly. "Finally."

"Do you know where he was going next?" asked Jack.

"Headed for the market, in a big hurry, as usual," said the blacksmith, nodding toward the street. Then he went back to pounding.

Jack and Annie ran up the street. They rounded a corner and stepped into a huge square. Sunlight shone down on hundreds of tents and stalls. The air smelled of fish and cinnamon and other spices.

"Oh, man," said Jack. "It's huge!"

The market was jam-packed with shoppers. It was hard to see over the heads of all the grown-ups. "We could spend all day looking for Leonardo here," said Jack.

"This is not good," said Annie. "We're

supposed to spend the day *helping* him, not *looking* for him! Remember the rhyme said, 'Help the genius all day long, morning, noon, and afternoon, till the night bird sings its song.'"

"Yeah, whatever *that* means," said Jack.

"Hey, maybe we should use the wand now," said Annie. "This situation fits the rules. Finding Leonardo is not just for *our* good—it's to help Merlin. And I think we've tried our hardest."

"Okay, let's use it." Jack slipped the Wand of Dianthus out of his bag and handed it to Annie. "Five words," he said.

"I know, I know," she said. She held up the wand and counted her words on her fingers: "Help. Us. Find. Leonardo. Now."

Jack and Annie held their breath and waited. But nothing changed. Everything around them looked exactly the same.

"It's not working," said Jack. "What did we do wrong?"

"I don't know," said Annie. "I used five words.

It's definitely good for others. Maybe we haven't really tried our hardest yet."

Jack sighed. "Okay, let's keep trying." He took back the wand and slipped it into his bag.

"Oh, look at the birds over there!" said Annie. She pulled Jack over to a stall that sold caged birds. Only one bird was singing: a brown bird with a reddish tail. He was very plain, but he sang beautifully with whistles and trills.

"Hi, you," said Annie.

The bird tilted his head and looked straight at Annie. He chirped softly.

"Come on, Annie, we can't waste time here," said Jack. "We have to keep looking for Leonardo."

"But didn't you hear his song?" said Annie. "He wants to fly away. He wants to be free."

Jack looked around for the bird seller. He was standing nearby talking to a customer. "Forget it, Annie. We don't have money to pay for him," said Jack.

"But he wants me to help him," said Annie. "I can feel it." She reached toward the cage door.

"Annie, don't!" said Jack.

But Annie unlatched the door. The bird hopped onto the ground.

"Oh, no!" said Jack. He grabbed for the bird, but he was too late. The brown bird was already flying away into the blue sky.

"Yay!" said Annie.

"Hey!" shouted the bird seller, rushing over to them. "Were you trying to steal my bird?"

"We weren't stealing him!" said Annie. "We were setting him free!"

The bird seller grabbed Jack by the arm. "You'll have to pay for him, then!" he barked.

"But . . . but . . . ," stammered Jack.

"Marco, unhand that boy!" a man's voice boomed.

Jack turned to see a tall man in a purple cloak and floppy blue cap. He had a long nose, bright, kind eyes with heavy eyebrows, and a flowing beard. He looked *exactly* like the man on the cover of their book.

"Leonardo!" said Annie. "The wand worked!"

CHAPTER THREE

Ten Types of Noses

"Let the boy go, Marco," Leonardo said again.

"But I caught him trying to steal my bird," said Marco.

"No, Marco. The girl said they were setting him free," said Leonardo. "And I believe her."

"Then let them pay me!" the bird seller said.

"We don't have any money," Annie said in a small voice.

"I will take care of it," said Leonardo. He put down the basket he was carrying. It was filled with flowers, cheese, and a loaf of bread. He pulled out a gold coin. The bird seller let go of Jack and took the coin.

"Marco, when I lay in my cradle as a child, a bird flew down and struck me with its tail," said Leonardo. "Ever since then, I have wished—"

"I know, I know," interrupted Marco, "to be a bird yourself. You have told me this many times, Leonardo." The bird seller turned away to help a customer.

Leonardo turned to Jack and Annie. "Yes," he said, "to be a bird myself—which is why I often buy birds from Marco and set them free. So you see, my friends, you and I are kindred spirits."

"Yes, we are!" said Annie, grinning.

"Thanks for helping us!" said Jack. He gave Leonardo a big smile. He wanted the great genius to like them so they could spend the whole day with him. "I'm Jack and this is my sister, Annie. Actually it was Annie who freed—"

But Leonardo didn't give Jack a chance to finish. He kept talking. "In truth, I love *all* creatures! Every bird and animal known to man—and even the ones *not* known!" He laughed heartily.

"Me too!" said Annie.

"Me too!" said Jack.

Leonardo picked up some bird feathers from the ground. "Ah, beautiful," he said, holding them up to the sun. "I will sketch these later." He tucked the feathers into his basket with the bread and cheese and flowers. "Well, I must be on my way now, friends," he said. "Good day!" Leonardo turned and began walking briskly away from the bird stand.

Oh, no! thought Jack.

Before he could think of anything to say, Annie shouted, "Mr. da Vinci! Leonardo!"

Leonardo looked back at her. "Yes?"

"Do you . . . um . . . do you need any help today?" Annie asked. "Jack and I would really, really like to help you . . . all day . . . somehow."

Jack was embarrassed. He was sure Leonardo

would say no. But to his surprise, the great genius was looking at them closely and tapping his chin. "Well . . . actually I am facing a great task this morning," he said with a smile. He nodded. "Yes. Perhaps you could be my apprentices—just for today."

"Great!" said Annie.

"What's an *apprentice*?" asked Jack.

"Apprentices help a master artist or skilled worker," said Leonardo. "They work hard and study hard in hopes they'll become masters themselves someday."

"Cool," said Jack.

"Come along, then!" said Leonardo. He started walking again. Jack and Annie hurried alongside him. They left the crowded market and started up a cobblestone street.

"Do you children live in Florence?" asked Leonardo.

"No, we're from . . . um . . . far away," said Jack.

"We're here on a mission," said Annie. "We're looking for the secret of happiness."

Leonardo smiled. "Ah, yes, I discovered that secret some time ago," he said.

"You did?" asked Jack.

"Yes, it's something I sought and now I have it," said Leonardo. "It's really quite simple."

"What is it?" said Jack.

"The secret of happiness is *fame*," said Leonardo.

"Really? Fame?" said Annie.

"Yes!" said Leonardo. "When I look into the eyes of complete strangers and see their awe and admiration—that makes me very happy!"

As Leonardo strode a few feet ahead of them, Annie looked at Jack. "Fame," she said. "I guess that's our answer."

"I don't know," said Jack in a soft voice. "Remember what the rhyme said: 'Though the question is quite simple, simple answers might be wrong.'"

"Oh, yeah!" said Annie. "And the rhyme says that to learn the answer, we have to stay with him all day."

"Yep," said Jack. He didn't mind that part. Spending the day with one of the most amazing geniuses who ever lived seemed like a great idea.

Jack and Annie followed Leonardo into a square with a huge cathedral. On the top of the building was the enormous eight-sided dome that they'd seen from the tree house. *How did anyone ever build that?* Jack wondered.

As hundreds of people moved about the square, Leonardo stopped. He stared into the crowd. "Oh! Oh!" he said.

"What? What?" asked Annie.

"I see an angel!" said Leonardo.

"An angel?" said Jack. He looked at the crowd. He didn't see any angels.

"Over there!" Leonardo pointed to a short, dark-haired girl standing by herself. The girl didn't look at all like an angel to Jack. She looked like an ordinary kid.

Leonardo put down his basket, untied a small book from his belt, and pulled out a piece of chalk. He started to draw. "I have been seeking an angel for one of my paintings," he murmured as he sketched the girl. "I think I may have found her."

In a moment, Leonardo was done. "There." He showed his sketch to Jack and Annie. With just a few quick lines, he had created an angel. The drawing looked just like the real girl, yet somehow she really did look like an angel now.

"That's the nicest angel I've ever seen," said Annie.

"Hmm, I don't know," said Leonardo. "I fear the nose is not quite right. I'm afraid I must keep looking." He tore the page out of his sketchbook. "Perhaps you and Jack would like to have this?"

"Oh . . . yes!" said Annie. "Thank you."

"I'll carry it," said Jack. He took the drawing from Leonardo and carefully slid it into his bag, between the pages of their research book.

Leonardo put away his chalk and sketchbook and picked up his basket. "Come along," he said.

Jack and Annie half walked and half ran, trying to keep up with Leonardo's long strides.

"When I travel through the streets, I am always gathering information," Leonardo said. "I observe like a scientist. For instance, after years of observation, I now know there are ten different types of noses."

"Really?" said Annie. She felt her nose.

"Yes," said Leonardo, "straight, round, pointed, flat, narrow. . . . Of course that is from the *side.* If you look people straight in the face, you will find *eleven* types of noses."

"No kidding," said Jack.

Jack tried to get a good look at the noses they passed. He saw flat ones, round ones, straight ones . . . but many were hard to describe.

"My observations have also led me to conclude that there are many more types of *mouths* than noses," said Leonardo. "But the *location* of every mouth is almost always the same. It is halfway between the base of the nose and the chin."

"Really?" said Annie. She held up two fingers, trying to measure the distance between her nose, mouth, and chin. "I think you're right, Leonardo."

"I study people's expressions and gestures," said Leonardo. "I study their hands, their eyes, their hair. But to be a truly great artist, you must learn to combine your observations with your imagination." Suddenly he stopped. "Look up, look up!"

Jack and Annie stopped and looked up.

"See the clouds?" said Leonardo.

A few billowy clouds dotted the sky.

"What do they look like to you?" asked Leonardo. "What sorts of things?"

Big white blobs, thought Jack.

"The biggest one looks sort of like a castle," said Annie.

"Good, good!" said Leonardo.

"And that little one looks like a dog's head," said Annie, "like a Scottie puppy."

A Scottie puppy? thought Jack. He squinted, trying to see a puppy.

"Excellent!" said Leonardo. "And you, Jack? What about that one?" He pointed at a long cloud. "What do you see?"

Jack studied it. "Uh . . . well, I guess it sort of looks like a boat," he said.

"Wonderful!" said Leonardo. "I get ideas for my paintings from everything! I look at a watermark on a wall and see an old woman's face. I look at a food stain on my tablecloth and see a horse! I study rain puddles and rocks and see oceans and mountains!"

"Oh, I do that kind of thing, too!" said Annie.

"I imagine that the very first drawing might have been a simple line drawn around the shadow of a man on the wall of a cave," said Leonardo.

"Wow," breathed Annie.

Pretty cool, thought Jack. He liked Leonardo's way of thinking.

"Listen now to the cathedral bells," said Leonardo.

Jack listened. The bells played notes that went up and down:

Bong-bing-bong-bing.
Bong-bing-bong-bing.

"I hear the bells' voices as if they were singing

to me," said Leonardo. "Can you hear what they are saying?"

Well . . . no, thought Jack. He just heard *bongs* and *bings.*

"They're saying: *You have much to do this Monday, Leonardo da Vinci! Get to work!*" Leonardo laughed. "So let us be on our way, my friends!" And the great genius took off, walking quickly through the streets of Florence.

CHAPTER FOUR

Battle Scene

Jack and Annie hurried to keep up with Leonardo. "So where are we going?" Annie asked.

"To the palace of the great council," said Leonardo. "I was hired to paint a fresco in the council hall. I have been working on it for months."

"What's a *fresco*?" asked Jack.

"It is a work of art painted onto a wall," said Leonardo. "One must spread plaster on the wall and then paint very quickly before it dries."

"Sounds like fun," said Annie.

"Not for me," said Leonardo. "I believe great art requires much thought. I like to paint slowly, and I change things as I go along. So for this fresco, I have invented a special oil paint that dries very slowly."

"Does it work?" said Jack.

"Too well," said Leonardo. "Now I have a new problem: Neither the plaster nor my oil paints have dried at all."

"Oh, no," said Annie.

"But today all will be well!" Leonardo said cheerfully. "I have a plan to speed up the drying process. This morning I will fix everything!"

Leonardo led Jack and Annie into a square with a large building. "There it is," he said. "The palace of the great council."

The palace looked like a fortress. It had rough-looking stone walls and a tower that rose high into the air.

"The palace is a very important place," said

Leonardo. "It is where the governing council of Florence meets. Come along." He opened one of the grand doors and guided Jack and Annie into a courtyard with a fountain. "This way to the council hall," he said, "and the latest work of Leonardo da Vinci."

Leonardo bounded up some steps and down a corridor. Jack and Annie hurried after him until he passed through another grand doorway and stopped.

Leonardo put down his basket and raised his hands. "My fresco," he said.

"Oh, man," breathed Jack.

They were in an enormous room with tall, arched windows and vast white walls. Several young men stood on a wooden platform on the far side of the room. On the wall above them was a giant painting of a battle scene. It showed a tangle of men on horseback, fighting over a flag.

The men in the painting seemed to be in a fury as they slashed at each other with their swords. Their faces were twisted, their mouths snarling. Even their horses looked wild and angry.

"The city has paid me to paint a scene from a battle once fought to defend Florence," said Leonardo. "They wanted me to paint a scene of glory. But I believe war is a beastly madness. I hope my painting shows that."

"Oh, it does," said Annie.

Jack nodded. It was the scariest painting he'd ever seen.

"Zorro!" called Leonardo.

One of the young men on the platform climbed

down a ladder and jumped to the floor. He was a sturdy-looking teenager with a red face and wavy black hair.

"Are things any better this morning?" asked Leonardo.

"No, the paint is still very damp to the touch," said Zorro.

"Then let us proceed with our plan," said Leonardo. "Did the pots arrive from the black-smith?"

"Yes, over there," said Zorro. He pointed at two large iron pots beneath the platform.

"And you brought the wood?" said Leonardo.

"Yes," said Zorro. He pointed to a pile of wood stacked against a wall.

Leonardo set down his basket and headed over to the platform.

"What's the plan, Leonardo?" asked Annie as she and Jack followed him.

"My apprentices and I will fill the pots with wood and lift them onto the platform," said

Leonardo. "Then we will light fires in them. The heat of the fires will quickly dry the fresco."

"How can we help?" asked Jack.

"Bring us some kindling," said Leonardo.

"No problem!" said Jack. He put down his bag, and he and Annie hurried to the wood stack.

"Kindling?" she said.

"Small pieces of wood," said Jack. "They catch fire first and help get the big pieces started."

Jack and Annie picked sticks and twigs from the wood stack. They carried the kindling back to Leonardo, and he dumped it into the iron pots. Zorro brought over some logs. Then he and Leonardo hooked the handles of the pots to a system of ropes and pulleys.

"Pull!" Leonardo shouted.

The apprentices on the platform pulled on the ropes. The heavy pots swung into the air.

"Steady! Steady!" Leonardo shouted.

The apprentices slowly hauled up the pots. Then they pulled them onto the platform and placed them in front of the fresco.

"Light the fires!" shouted Leonardo.

Zorro lit a candle from a torch burning at the entrance of the hall. He carried the candle up the ladder and used its fire to light the kindling. Soon the wood in the pots began to blaze.

"Bring more wood!" Leonardo shouted. "Bring more wood!"

Jack and Annie hurried back to the woodpile. They gathered bigger pieces of wood and rushed back to the ladder. Apprentices lifted the wood up to the platform and added it to the fires in the pots.

Soon flames were shooting high into the air, warming the fresco. Standing with Leonardo below the platform, Jack and Annie stared up at the battle scene. The room grew hotter and hotter.

With the fires blazing above and smoke curling through the air, Jack felt like he was in the middle of the battle himself. He could hear the clanging swords, neighing horses, and shouting men. He could feel the "beastly madness" of war that Leonardo had talked about.

Suddenly Jack heard *real* shrieks—Leonardo's apprentices were all yelling.

"It is *dripping,* Master!" one cried.

"The paint is running!" shouted another.

Jack looked back at the fresco. The helmets of the warriors were melting down over their furious faces.

"AHHH!" cried Leonardo with a look of horror. "Kill the fires! Kill the fires!"

CHAPTER FIVE

Knock, Knock

The panic of the battle scene seemed to spread through the big room. Leonardo's apprentices looked around wildly, as if they didn't know what to do.

"Water from the fountain!" Leonardo roared. "Hurry!" He ran out of the room. His apprentices rushed after him.

"We have to help, too!" Jack said to Annie. They took off after the others, following them down the stairs to the courtyard.

The apprentices were filling buckets with

water from the fountain. "Hurry! Hurry! Hurry!"
Leonardo shouted.

Jack and Annie grabbed two of the full buckets and clumsily followed the others back up the

stairs. "This is like—like Edo!" Jack said to Annie, remembering their recent trip to old Japan.

"Yeah," said Annie, "except that was a *city* on fire. This is just paint melting."

True, thought Jack. But Leonardo was acting like it was a matter of life and death.

Inside the hall, Leonardo and the apprentices carried the buckets up the ladder. They splashed water over the flames in the two iron pots. But it was too late. The helmets and faces and swords of the fighting men had become a messy blur of streaks and blotches. The painting was ruined.

Leonardo stared for a long moment at the wall. Then he climbed down the ladder and walked away. When he got to the door, Zorro shouted, "Master, wait!" But Leonardo kept walking.

"We have to follow him," Annie said to Jack.

"He seems really upset," said Jack.

"I know," said Annie. "But we have to do what the rhyme says—'*Help the genius all day long.*'"

"But what if he doesn't want our help any-more?" said Jack.

"Look! He forgot his basket, with all his stuff in it," said Annie. "We can take it to him."

"Okay. Good," said Jack.

Annie picked up Leonardo's basket filled with feathers, flowers, cheese, and a loaf of bread. Jack grabbed his own bag and they hurried out of the council hall. When they got to the entrance of the palace, they saw Leonardo striding across the square.

"Leonardo!" Annie yelled.

Leonardo didn't look back. He disappeared down a narrow lane.

"Quick!" said Jack.

Jack and Annie took off across the square. When they got to the lane, they saw Leonardo at the far end.

"Leonardo, wait!" Annie shouted.

But Leonardo didn't wait. He kept going and rounded a corner.

Annie and Jack ran faster. When they turned the corne they looked right and left. Kids were playing in the street. Two women were leaning out of windows talking to each other. But there was no sign of Leonardo.

"Excuse me," Annie called to the women. "Have you seen Leonardo da Vinci?"

"Oh, yes, he just got home!" one woman said.

"He lives just over there!" said her neighbor. She pointed to a narrow building across the street.

"Thank you!" said Annie. She and Jack walked quickly to the building. A stone arch opened onto a wide pathway. They walked under the arch and down the pathway to a sunny cobblestone courtyard. A big white horse was tied to a cart. Chickens pecked the dirt between the warm stones.

"Hi, guys," Annie said to the horse and chickens.

Jack pointed to an open doorway across the yard. "He's in there. I hear him," he said.

Annie and Jack moved quietly across the courtyard. They stopped outside a window.

Leonardo was pacing up and down inside. His cap and cloak were on the floor. His hair was wild.

"I'll leave Florence—that's what I'll do," Leonardo said to himself. "I shall go to Rome! Or back to Milan!"

Jack turned to Annie. "We shouldn't bother him," he whispered. "If *I* felt that bad, I wouldn't want people to bother me."

"Not *bother*," said Annie. "*Help*. If I felt that bad, I'd want people to *help* me. Come on, at least we can give him his stuff." Before Jack could stop her, Annie stepped into Leonardo's room. "Knock, knock," she said loudly.

Leonardo whirled around. His face was red. He was scowling. "What are *you* doing here?" he said.

"We brought your things," said Annie. "You forgot them." She held up the basket.

"Oh." Leonardo's face softened. "Thank you. Leave it all by the door, please," he said.

Annie put the basket down. Then she looked up at Leonardo.

"We'd better go," Jack said softly to her.

"Wait." Annie stepped farther into Leonardo's room. "We'd like to help you," she said.

Leonardo scowled again. "You cannot help me," he said. "Do as your brother says, little girl. Go now."

But Annie didn't move. "Excuse me, but we're supposed to help you all day," she said. "You made us your apprentices for the day, remember?"

"Can you not see that I am miserable?" said Leonardo.

"But *why* are you miserable?" said Annie. "You said that fame was the secret of happiness. And you're still famous."

"But what good is fame in the face of failure?" shouted Leonardo. "This fresco was to be my masterpiece! What good is fame when everyone will now laugh at me and mock my failure? Go! Please!"

"Oh, okay. I'm sorry," said Annie in a small

voice. "We just wanted to help." She and Jack turned to go.

"Wait, wait, wait," said Leonardo. "Forgive me."

Jack and Annie looked back at Leonardo. The great genius rubbed his face and sighed. Then he waved his hand. "Please, forgive me. Come in, come in," he said.

"Thanks," said Annie. And she and Jack stepped inside Leonardo da Vinci's studio.

CHAPTER SIX

Thousands of Ideas

A low fire burned in the hearth. Sunlight slanted across the warm room. Jack caught his breath as he looked around Leonardo's studio.

There were mirrors, wooden trunks, globes, paint pots, and brushes. Sketches, paintings, and handmade maps were all over the walls. There were stacks of old books, half-built furniture, piled-up papers, theater masks, pieces of costumes, and musical instruments.

"Oh, man," murmured Jack, "I *love* this room."

"Me too," said Annie.

"Please, sit at my table. Let me get you something to eat," said Leonardo. He pushed a bunch of things to the side of a long wooden table and pulled up two chairs.

"Thanks," said Jack. He and Annie sat down.

Leonardo took the cheese and bread from the basket by the door and gave some to Jack and Annie. The cheese was dry but tasted good. And the bread was *really* delicious—hard and crackly on the outside, but soft and chewy on the inside. *Hmm, I wonder how they make it like this*, Jack thought.

"So why do you want to leave Florence, Leonardo?" Annie asked, her mouth full.

"Because I will no longer be respected here," said Leonardo. "Last week, the council told me I must finish my fresco soon. And now I will not finish it at all. Just recently Michelangelo accused me of never finishing *anything*!"

"Michelangelo? The great artist?" said Jack.

Leonardo snorted. "You think Michelangelo is a great artist? Have you seen his statues? Those men with their big muscles? They look like sacks of walnuts!"

Jack and Annie laughed.

Leonardo tried to hide a smile as he looked at them. "In truth, Michelangelo *is* a great artist," he said. "Still, he should not accuse me of never finishing anything . . . even if it is true."

"Why don't you finish things?" asked Annie.

"Well, I shall not finish my battle scene now because I experimented with my paint," said Leonardo. "I am experimenting all the time. And often my experiments lead nowhere."

"So is that your main problem?" asked Annie.

"One of them," said Leonardo, sighing. "The other is that there are too many things I want to do, and there is never enough time!"

"What else do you want to do?" asked Jack.

"Oh, I have thousands of ideas," said Leonardo. He put down his bread and cheese and crossed to a wooden trunk in the corner of his studio. He raised the lid of the trunk and stared for a moment at its contents.

Leonardo turned back to Jack and Annie. His eyes were bright again. Whatever was in the trunk had made him happier. "Come, look," he said.

Jack and Annie walked over to the trunk and peered inside. It held dozens and dozens of plain black books, large ones and small ones.

"Notebooks," said Leonardo. "I have filled over a hundred of them with my ideas."

"Oh," said Jack, his eyes wide.

"Jack keeps notebooks, too!" said Annie.

"Do you mind if we look at them?" asked Jack.

"No, not at all," said Leonardo.

Jack and Annie started picking up the notebooks and turning the pages. The pages were crammed with doodles and writing. They showed sketches of people's faces, animal heads, flowers, trees, rivers, mountains, the sun, and the moon.

One notebook was filled with drawings of horses. Another had sketches of bridges and buildings. Another had drawings of birds and machines. Many of the drawings in the notebooks had labels written in a strange language.

"You cannot read my notes, can you?" said Leonardo.

Jack and Annie shook their heads.

"Hold them to a mirror," said Leonardo.

Jack and Annie stood in front of a wall mirror.

Each held up a notebook and looked at its reflection in the mirror.

"Oh, I get it!" said Jack. He could read the words now! Leonardo had written everything backward—from right to left across the page. So the word *bird* was written as bɿid, and the word *wind* was written as bniw.

"Why do you write this way?" asked Annie.

"People think I am trying to keep my ideas a secret," said Leonardo. "But, in truth, I am left-handed, and when I write normally from left to right, I smear ink across the page. One day I realized that if I wrote backward, I would not be so messy." He laughed and sat down at the table. As he took a bite of bread, he seemed his happy self again.

"What do you write in these notebooks?" said Jack.

"Oh, I've written down thousands of ideas," said Leonardo. "For example—" He opened a notebook and read: *Fossils of tiny sea creatures have been found in the mountains of Italy. It is my belief that ocean water once covered the mountains millions of years ago."*

"Your belief is right," said Jack.

Leonardo looked at Jack with surprise. "You seem so certain," he said.

"Well, I know from science books that the oceans once covered many mountains of the earth, and that's why you can find sea fossils there," said Jack.

"We read lots of books," said Annie.

"Indeed?" said Leonardo. Then he picked up another notebook and read: *"If a wolf stares at you, your voice will become hoarse."*

"Um . . . that's not true," said Annie.

"It is not?" said Leonardo.

"Well, think about it," said Annie. "How could an animal make a person hoarse? And why would they want to?"

Leonardo nodded. "Yes, I think I agree with you," he said. He cleared his throat. Then he read another idea: *"A spider hatches its eggs by staring at them."*

"Nooo," said Jack and Annie together.

"No?" said Leonardo.

"Trust us," said Jack, smiling. *This is really fun,* he thought, *knowing more than a great genius. Scientists have discovered a lot since Leonardo's time.*

"All right. I don't know why, but I shall trust you," said Leonardo. He turned some pages and read: *"The moon may be bright because it is made out of rippling water."*

Jack shook his head. "Actually it's made out of rocks," he said. "It's bright because it reflects the light of the sun." Jack knew lots of facts about the moon.

"And did you know there's no wind on the moon?" said Annie. "So someday when people walk there, their footprints will last forever!"

Leonardo grinned. "Wonderful," he said. "I fear you are both speaking nonsense. But I like your original thinking!"

He turned the page and read another entry:

"There must be a way to use a natural force, such as steam or wind, to help people do their tasks in less time, with less work—"

"That's a great idea," said Jack. "Maybe someday *steam* engines could run ships. Or maybe steam could help run a train."

"A train?" said Leonardo.

"Yes, a train!" said Annie. "A train is this thing we've imagined. It's like—um—"

"Like wagons connected to each other!" said Jack. "And they run over tracks that go across the land."

"Interesting," said Leonardo. He closed his eyes as if trying to imagine it.

"And then there are *planes*," said Annie. "We've imagined these things called planes."

"Yeah," said Jack, "they have wings, and they fly you through the air."

"Like birds!" said Annie.

Leonardo sat up very straight. "You imagine such a flying thing is possible?" he asked.

"We're positive," said Jack.

Leonardo leapt to his feet. "You have been sent to me as a sign!" he said.

"A sign of what?" said Annie.

Leonardo's eyes were gleaming. "I, too, believe humans can fly like birds. And today I shall prove it!"

"You will?" said Jack.

"Yes! Until now, I have been fearful of testing my idea," said Leonardo. "But the two of you have given me courage!"

What is Leonardo talking about? Jack wondered.

"I am sure my plan will work now!" said Leonardo. "And it will bring me everlasting fame!"

"We don't really know *that* much about flying," Jack said.

"Yeah, we were just *imagining*," said Annie.

But Leonardo had grabbed his cap and cloak. "Come with me, friends!" He headed out to the courtyard.

Jack grabbed his bag, and he and Annie followed. Leonardo jumped into the horse cart and picked up the reins. "Climb in! Climb in!" he said.

Jack and Annie climbed into the cart and sat beside Leonardo.

"Today the Great Bird shall rise aloft high into the sky!" said Leonardo. "And the universe shall be filled with wonder!"

CHAPTER SEVEN

The Great Bird

Leonardo shook the reins. The white horse clopped out of the courtyard and into the street.

"So where are we going?" Annie asked.

"To a steep hill just outside the city walls," said Leonardo. "One day you will tell people that you were with me on this historic Monday. You saw the mad genius, Leonardo da Vinci, and his Great Bird!"

"Cool, but can you tell us exactly what you're planning to do?" said Jack.

"For twenty-five years, I have sketched birds

and bats," said Leonardo. "I have studied all their movements, their gliding, their flapping, their landing, and their rising into the air. I have asked myself over and over, *Why can a person not fly as birds do?* So, years ago I began building my Great Bird."

"Your Great Bird?" asked Annie.

"Ha-ha!" laughed Leonardo. "Wait and see! Wait and see!"

The horse pulled the cart through the city gates, heading into the countryside. The chilly air was warmed by bright sunlight.

Leonardo tugged on the reins and his horse turned off the main road and started up a narrow, rocky path. The cart bumped past pale green olive trees and yellow fields of wildflowers. Soon it came to the bottom of a steep hill.

Leonardo pulled the reins and his horse halted. "There! Can you see it?" he said. "My Great Bird." He pointed to a strange-looking structure on the top of the hill.

"What is it?" asked Jack.

"The wings are like those of a bat, only much, much larger—large enough for a man!" said Leonardo. "About a month ago on a moonlit night, my apprentices and I brought it to the top of this hill. I did not have the confidence to try it then, but now I do."

Jack was confused. He knew people didn't fly airplanes until the beginning of the 1900s. "Um—maybe you should work on this one a little longer," he said. "I mean, maybe—"

"No, no, today is the day! I feel it!" said Leonardo. "Stay here and watch."

Leonardo leapt down from the cart and took long strides up the steep slope.

"Quick, look up *Great Bird* in the Leonardo book," Annie said to Jack.

Jack pulled out their research book and looked up *Great Bird* in the index. "It's here!" he said. He found the right page and read aloud:

Leonardo da Vinci spent years making a flying machine that he called the Great Bird. But not until the invention of lightweight motors, nearly 400 years after Leonardo's time, would human flight be possible. It is not known whether Leonardo ever tried to fly the Great Bird. If he did, he surely crashed.

"Oh, no!" said Annie. "His machine won't work! If Leonardo tries to fly off that hilltop, he'll crash. We have to stop him before he hurts himself!"

Annie jumped out of the cart. Jack put the book away. He left his bag in the cart and ran after her. They started up the steep hill.

"Leonardo, stop!" shouted Annie.

But Leonardo kept climbing.

"Human flight isn't possible yet!" Jack cried.

"Don't try it, Leonardo!" yelled Annie.

Jack and Annie were only halfway up the hill when Leonardo reached the top. He began strapping himself into a harness on the Great Bird.

Large handles were attached to the harness. On each side were huge cloth wings stretched over a wooden frame.

"Don't!" shouted Jack.

But Leonardo was already staggering toward the edge of the steep hill with the flying machine on his back. It was so heavy that he could hardly stand up.

"Leonardo, stop!" cried Annie. "You need a motor!"

But Leonardo bent his legs and lowered his body close to the ground. He grabbed the two large handles and pulled them toward his chest. The huge wings rose into the air.

"The Great Bird raises its wings and is pushed by the wind!" shouted Leonardo.

"Noooo!" yelled Jack and Annie.

Leonardo leapt off the side of the hill into the air. A gust of wind lifted him. As the wind held his wings aloft, he pushed and pulled on the handles. The wings moved up and down.

But Leonardo couldn't make the wings flap fast enough. Though he pushed and pulled wildly on the handles, he soon began falling through the air—until wings and wood and Leonardo all crashed to the ground.

"Leonardo!" yelled Annie.

Jack and Annie charged down the hill. At the bottom, Leonardo da Vinci lay in a silent heap. His twisted wings spread over the grass. Jack and Annie rushed to him.

"Are you all right?" cried Annie.

There was no answer.

Oh, no! We've killed him! thought Jack.

But then Leonardo stirred. He moved his hand.

"Are you all right?" Annie asked again.

Leonardo moved his other hand. He rolled over on his side and unbuckled the straps of the harness. He crawled away from the flying machine and hauled himself to a sitting position. His face was scraped and red.

"Are you all right?" Annie asked once more.

Leonardo looked at her. The light had gone out of his eyes. "No," he said in a quiet voice. "I am *not* all right."

"Did you break something?" asked Annie.

Leonardo stood up. He stared at the twisted and torn wings of the Great Bird. He sighed deeply. "Only my heart," he said. "Only my heart."

Leonardo turned and limped across the grass back toward his horse and cart. Jack and Annie followed. When Leonardo got to the cart, his white horse snorted, as if trying to comfort him. Leonardo pressed his head against the horse's neck.

Annie stepped toward him. "Why is your heart broken, Leonardo?" she asked quietly.

Leonardo looked back at the hill. "All my life, I have started projects that have come to nothing," he said. "My towers and bridges have never been built. My scientific ideas have never been proven."

"But—" said Annie.

Leonardo went on: "For years, I made drawings of an enormous horse I planned to sculpt for the Duke of Milan. But in the end, that work came to nothing, too. I have finished only a few paintings. I cannot even finish my favorite one, a portrait of a lovely lady of Florence. Today my fresco in the hall of the great council was ruined. But always, in spite of all my failures, one thing brought me comfort."

"What?" asked Jack.

"I knew someday I would be the first person in the world to fly," said Leonardo. His voice quavered. "Talking with the two of you, I knew the time had finally come to test my machine."

"We're sorry," said Annie.

"No, no, I had to test it sooner or later," said Leonardo. "But now that dream, too, has come to nothing. I will never achieve fame by flying. I will never fly." He hung his head and stared at the ground. "I shall go home now. I shall burn all my notebooks and my unfinished paintings and inventions. I shall leave Florence and never return."

"Oh, no!" said Jack.

"Wait a minute," said Annie. "You *will* fly."

"*Annie,*" Jack warned. Since the machine would never work, he didn't want her to give Leonardo false hope.

"You *are* going to fly, Leonardo," said Annie. "And you're going to love it."

"Annie, human flight isn't possible at this time in history!" Jack whispered to Annie. "A person needs a motor. We don't have a motor."

But Annie paid no attention. "Hold on, everyone," she said. "I have to get something." She climbed into the cart and reached into Jack's bag.

When Annie turned back around, Jack gasped. He had forgotten all about the Wand of Dianthus.

CHAPTER EIGHT

Wings!

Annie held up the wand. "Close your eyes, Leonardo," she said.

Leonardo just shook his head.

"Please?" said Annie. "Just for a second?"

Leonardo put his head in his hands.

"Listen," said Annie. "This morning you said that a great artist has to combine observation with imagination."

Leonardo barely nodded.

"Well, watch out—because *this* is the imagination part!" said Annie. She waved the wand at

Leonardo, then at herself and Jack. Counting her words on her fingers, she said in a loud, clear voice: "Make. Us. Fly. Like. Birds."

Leonardo's arms whipped out to his sides. They sprouted long grayish feathers. He let out a yelp. The next thing Jack knew, *his* arms had turned into feathery wings, too! So had Annie's!

"What's happening?" cried Leonardo.

"Wings!" said Annie.

Jack's wings felt light and airy, yet strong and powerful.

"Now we can fly!" said Annie.

"Wings?" said Leonardo, looking stunned. Then he burst out laughing. "We have wings! We have wings! Run! Run into the wind!"

Jack, Annie, and Leonardo all stretched out their wings and took quick steps forward. The wind rushed under their feathers and lifted them off the ground.

"WHOOOAH!" cried Leonardo.

Leonardo, Jack, and Annie flapped their

wings and soared high into the sky. Then they caught a gentle wind and stopped flapping. Twisting this way and that, they glided in a big circle above the countryside.

Jack felt as light as the wind. His heart beat wildly.

"Incredible, huh?" yelled Annie.

"Best flying ever!" shouted Jack.

Jack and Annie had flown lots before. They'd flown on a dragon, on a bicycle, on a winged lion, on a magic carpet, and on the back of a white stag in Camelot. They'd even flown as ravens over a haunted castle. But this was the first time they'd ever flown on their own, just as themselves.

"Follow me!" cried Leonardo. He tilted his wings and flew out of the circle. Jack and Annie flew after him. They all swooped high up over the quiet hills and glided through low clouds.

The cool, wet mist blew against Jack's face. He felt as if he were swimming through the sky, as if the clouds were water keeping him afloat.

Laughing and whooping with delight, Leonardo led Jack and Annie out of the clouds and down over the yellow meadows and the pale green olive groves.

"Helloooo!" Leonardo shouted to farmers plowing a field. But the farmers didn't look up.

"Helloooo!" he called to grape pickers working in a vineyard, but they didn't look up, either.

No one on the ground looked up, but all the birds in the sky seemed to take notice. Birds cawed and swooped near them, as if welcoming them to their world. Birds flew alongside them and spread out in front of them, leading them over the city walls of Florence.

Jack, Annie, and Leonardo circled with the birds over the sea of red-tiled roofs, over the great dome of the cathedral, and over the bell tower of the palace of the great council.

"Florence looks so neat and orderly from up here!" Leonardo cried to Jack and Annie. "I wish I had my sketchbook!"

The city *did* look orderly from the sky, thought Jack:

the busy market

with its rows of stalls and tents,

the narrow lanes with the brightly colored

clothes waving from clotheslines,

the long covered bridge,

the winding, sparkling river.

Jack, Annie, and Leonardo soared with the birds back over the city walls out to the countryside. They glided over the olive groves and vineyards. Then they circled above the spot where Leonardo's Great Bird lay broken in the grass.

The birds swooped up and vanished behind the clouds. Leonardo, Jack, and Annie glided down toward the ground. They opened their wings wide and then, gently and easily, their feet touched the grass. Their wings fluttered with tiny beats, and the three of them took quick hopping steps before coming to a full stop.

When Jack, Annie, and Leonardo were steady

on their feet, their long feathers disappeared and their bird wings became arms again. Leonardo looked dazed. He stared up at the sky. Then he staggered a few steps and fell facedown into the grass.

"Leonardo?" said Annie.

Oh, no, thought Jack. *He's had a heart attack.*

"Leonardo?" said Annie. She knelt down near him.

Leonardo rolled over and stared up at Jack and Annie. "What . . . what just happened?" he stammered. "Did we fly? Did we really fly? Or was it a dream?"

"Uh . . . well . . ." Jack didn't know what to say. To explain the wand to Leonardo, they'd have to start way back at the very beginning—with the tree house, Morgan, Merlin, Teddy, Kathleen, Dianthus. It would take forever.

"Well," said Annie. "One day a long time ago, we were playing in the woods and we saw—"

"Annie—" Jack shook his head.

Annie frowned. "I guess it can't really be explained," she said.

Leonardo looked up at the sky. "No, no," he said. "I think you are right. Perhaps some things should remain mysteries and are better kept in our hearts. We should not try to explain them."

That's an amazing statement, Jack thought, *from a person who always tries to explain everything.*

"But if I *had* to explain it, I would explain it *this* way," said Leonardo. He leapt to his feet. "For years, I wrote down all my observations of bird flight. I made hundreds of drawings. These things helped me build my flying machine. But in the end, something was missing—something very important."

"What?" asked Annie.

"The *spirit* of a bird!" said Leonardo. "A bird is not just a machine. A bird has a spirit. And with the two of you, I somehow gained that spirit. If only for a short time and if only in my imagination, we all became more bird than human!"

"And did the spirit of the bird mend your heart?" Annie asked.

Leonardo smiled. "Yes, my heart is mended now. I am ready to leave this dream behind and move on to others. And it does not matter that the world will never know of my great triumph."

"So maybe fame *isn't* the secret of happiness?" said Jack.

"Absolutely not," said Leonardo. "I know that now. We must do what we do to satisfy our own hearts. For instance, I am working on a painting now. I love it. I do not care if others ever see it. . . . Oh! Oh, no! What time is it?" He jerked his head around to look at the sun. "I must go! I will be late!"

"Late for what?" said Annie.

"To meet my model at the studio!" said Leonardo. "The woman I am painting in the portrait I was just talking about! We must return!"

Jack, Annie, and Leonardo hurried back to the cart and climbed in. Leonardo snapped the reins, and the white horse started clopping back toward Florence.

CHAPTER NINE

The Smile

At first no one spoke on the trip back. It was as if they didn't want to break the spell of joy that had settled over them. Even though Jack was bumping up and down in the cart, he could still remember the feeling of flying smoothly through the sky. He could feel the wind rustling his long feathers.

The cart passed through a gate in the city walls. As they started through the streets, Annie broke the silence. "So if fame is *not* the secret of happiness," she said to Leonardo, "then what *is*? Do you think it could be *flying*?"

Leonardo thought for a moment. "No, no. The secret of happiness cannot be flying," he said.

"Why not?" asked Jack.

"Because flying is a great dream that no one but us will ever realize," said Leonardo. "Surely happiness cannot be only for *us*."

"True," said Annie.

"So what *do* you think the secret is?" asked Jack.

"Hmm . . ." Leonardo was silent. Then he sighed. "I must think about it," he said.

Jack looked worriedly at the sky. The sun would go down soon and night would come. According to their rhyme, they were supposed to leave when the night bird sang its song. "Um . . . how long do you think it'll take you to think about it?" Jack asked.

"I do not know," said Leonardo. "Right now all I know is that I must hurry to meet with my model. She is already unhappy enough without my being late."

"Why is she unhappy?" asked Annie.

"She will not say," said Leonardo. "Perhaps she is tired of posing for me. For three years, she has been sitting for her portrait."

"Whoa, that's a really long time," said Annie, "especially if you're just sitting."

"Yes, yes, it is," said Leonardo. "Lately she will not even smile. She only stares at me sadly. I have tried hiring singers, musicians, and jokesters to amuse her, but nothing helps."

"Maybe you shouldn't meet with her today," said Jack. He didn't want Leonardo to lose his good feelings from flying. And he wanted him to spend time thinking about the secret of happiness.

"No, I must," said Leonardo. "The light is perfect today. Late afternoon is the best time for painting a portrait—in my courtyard, when the sunlight is golden and shadows are beginning to fall."

Shadows *were* falling as the white horse pulled the cart into Leonardo's courtyard. A young woman was standing by the studio door.

"Lisa!" called Leonardo.

"Hello, Leonardo," the woman said. She wore a dark gown with a silk cloth over her shoulder. A thin veil covered her long brown hair. She had a high forehead and large brown eyes. Oddly, she looked like someone Jack knew, but he couldn't remember who.

"Forgive me, Lisa. I am late," said Leonardo, leaping down from the cart. "Will you wait for me to set up my things?"

"Yes, I will wait," said Lisa.

Leonardo hurried inside, and Jack and Annie climbed down from the cart. "Hi, we're Annie and Jack," said Annie.

The woman smiled at them. "I am Lisa," she said.

"You look familiar to me," said Annie.

"Really?" said Lisa. "Are you from Florence?"

"No, we're from Frog Creek, Pennsylvania," said Annie. "It's far away."

Lisa smiled again. "I like the name of your town," she said.

So Lisa *did* smile for other people, thought Jack. He wondered why she wouldn't smile for Leonardo.

Leonardo came back outside, carrying a small canvas, an easel, and a paint box. He then brought out a stool for Lisa. She sat down and folded her hands.

Leonardo placed the canvas on his easel. As he prepared his paints, Jack and Annie looked at his painting-in-progress.

"Nice," breathed Annie.

The small canvas showed the model, Lisa. Except for her mouth, her whole face had been painted. In the background was a misty landscape with mountains and winding rivers.

Leonardo picked up his brush, dipped it into a paint jar, and began to work. Jack and Annie watched closely as the great genius brushed a thin coat of green paint over the scenery.

"What are you doing now?" whispered Annie.

"I paint many very thin coats over the background," murmured Leonardo. "This casts a soft green light over everything. So it all blends together like smoke, and you cannot tell light from shadow."

"How'd you figure that out?" asked Annie. "I mean, you're always coming up with new ways to do things. How do you do that?"

"I ask questions," said Leonardo. "All the time, I ask questions: How can I paint the light? How can I capture the shadows? How can I do this? How can I do that?" Leonardo stopped painting. He put down his brush and looked at Jack and Annie. His eyes were sparkling. "And now, my friends, I know the secret."

"You do?" said Jack.

"Yes," said Leonardo. "The secret of happiness is available to *all* of us, *every* hour of *every* day. Young, old, rich, poor—*everyone* can choose to find happiness in this way."

"How?" asked Annie. "What's the secret?" She and Jack leaned forward, eager to hear the answer.

"*Curiosity,*" said Leonardo.

"Curiosity?" repeated Jack. He had curiosity. He had lots of it.

"Always ask questions," said Leonardo. "Always try to learn something new. Ask: Why? When? Where? What? Say: 'I wonder what this means.' 'I wonder how that works.' 'I wonder what this person is like. And that person. And that one.' I am always searching for answers to things I do not understand."

"Me too!" said Jack.

"And so I look forward to each new day, each spring and summer and fall and winter, and all the months and years ahead, because there is so much to discover," said Leonardo.

"Me too!" said Annie.

"Through my curiosity, I forget my failures and sorrows, and I feel great happiness," said Leonardo. He looked up at the sky. "For instance, one might wonder how they built that eight-sided dome on top of the cathedral."

"I *do* wonder that!" said Jack.

"And I wonder—what exactly makes the clouds change shape?" said Annie.

"And—and what makes bread crackly on the outside and soft on the inside?" asked Jack.

"Are there really just ten types of noses?" said Annie.

"How many kinds of ears are there?" said Jack. "How many kinds of feet?"

"Hands!" said Annie.

"Eyebrows!" said Jack.

Their two voices spilled over each other as they kept calling out questions: "And who rings the bells in the bell tower?" "Why is the sky blue?" "Where do city birds sleep?"

"AND WHY WON'T LISA SMILE FOR LEONARDO?" asked Annie.

Jack and Leonardo looked at Annie. Then they all turned and looked at Lisa. Jack had actually forgotten she was sitting near them.

The quiet, lovely woman blinked. "What?" she said. "What did you say?"

"Why won't you smile for Leonardo, Lisa?" asked Annie. "Are you mad at him because you've been posing for three years?"

Lisa's face grew red. She seemed to be fighting tears. She shook her head.

"Is—is there another reason?" Annie asked softly.

Lisa looked at Leonardo. He was staring back at her. "Yes," she whispered. "There is."

"What is it?" Annie asked.

"I am afraid to smile," said Lisa. She kept staring at Leonardo, though she was talking to Annie. "If I smile, Leonardo will paint my smile, and he will be done with me. He will sell my portrait to my family and never think of me again."

There was silence for a moment. Jack and Annie looked at Leonardo. "Annie," said Leonardo finally, staring at Lisa. "Tell Lisa that if she will smile, I *will* finish her portrait. But tell her that I *will not* sell it to her family. I will carry it with me wherever I go, for the rest of my life, and I will never forget her."

"Lisa, Leonardo says that—" started Annie.

But Lisa stopped her. "I heard," she said softly. Then she smiled. It was a faint smile, but a mysterious and beautiful one. Her face glowed in the golden light of late afternoon.

"Ah!" gasped Leonardo. "Keep that smile," he said. He kept staring at Lisa as he dipped his paintbrush into a jar. "Please! Keep that smile, Mona Lisa."

Mona Lisa? Jack had heard the name Mona Lisa before.

Lisa kept smiling. Leonardo painted.

"Hey, listen," Annie said to Jack.

Jack listened. He heard a bird whistling and trilling. A plain brown bird was singing from the rooftop above the courtyard.

"That looks like the bird you let out of the cage," said Jack.

"It *is* him!" whispered Annie.

"He is a nightingale," said Leonardo, keeping his eyes on Lisa. "A beautiful singer, yes?"

Annie smiled at Jack. "Time to go," she said. "Remember Morgan's rhyme—help the genius *'Till the night bird sings its song.'*"

"Right," said Jack, sighing. "Good-bye, Leonardo."

Leonardo didn't seem to hear him.

"Good-bye, Lisa," said Annie.

Lisa turned her eyes to look at Jack and Annie. "Bye," she whispered.

Then Leonardo turned and looked at them, too. "Yes, good-bye, my friends!" he said. "Come again soon, please! You have been a great help to me today."

"You helped us, too," said Annie.

Leonardo bowed to them. Then he turned back to his work. He painted Lisa's smile as the nightingale sang on. The bird's song grew louder and louder, until it seemed to fill the Florence night.

CHAPTER TEN

Questions

It was twilight when Annie and Jack stepped back out into the street.

"Where's the tree with the tree house?" asked Annie.

"Somewhere over the bridge beyond the big dome," said Jack.

They kept their eyes on the dome as they threaded their way through the streets of Florence. When they came to the cathedral, the square was quiet. The cathedral's great doors were open. Jack and Annie could see candles burning inside.

Jack and Annie kept walking and soon came to the market. The hundreds of tents and stalls were all closed for the night. The square was empty.

Jack and Annie returned the way they had come that morning. Walking down the same narrow lanes, they saw that all the shops were closed now, too. They crossed the covered bridge and walked along the flowing river, past quiet houses where smoke curled from chimneys into the darkening sky.

Finally Jack and Annie came to the hedge that hid the tree with the tree house. In the gray light of dusk, they climbed up the rope ladder.

"Before we go home, I want to look something up," said Jack. He pulled their research book out of his bag and looked in the index for *Mona Lisa*. He found it and turned to the right page.

"Look! It's Lisa!" said Annie.

Jack and Annie stared at a picture of Leonardo's painting. It looked exactly the same, except now there was a smile on Lisa's face, the same smile they'd just seen in real life. Jack read aloud:

> Leonardo da Vinci's painting of Mona Lisa is perhaps the most famous painting in the world. It is believed to be a portrait of Lisa del Gioconda. (The Italian word *mona* means "my lady.") Leonardo da Vinci never sold the portrait of Lisa. He took it with him everywhere he traveled until he died.

Jack closed the book. "He kept his promise," he said.

"I knew he would," said Annie. She sighed. "Good-bye, Leonardo," she whispered. Then she picked up their note from Morgan and pointed at the words *Frog Creek*. "I wish we could go there," she said.

The wind started to blow.

The tree house started to spin.

It spun faster and faster.

Then everything was still.

Absolutely still.

Sunlight flooded through the tree house window. No time had passed in Frog Creek. The school bell was still ringing, announcing that class would start in ten minutes. Jack and Annie were wearing their school clothes. Jack's cloth bag had changed back into his backpack.

"We have to hurry," said Annie.

"I know," said Jack. He looked inside his pack.

He was happy to see the Wand of Dianthus. As he pulled out their research book, a piece of paper fell out. It was the sketch of Leonardo's angel.

"Oh, I forgot all about this," said Jack. He and Annie looked at the sketch.

"It shows he was really a good drawer," said Annie.

"Yep," said Jack. "And it will remind us about Leonardo's secret of happiness."

"He was curious about everything," said Annie. "Angels, noses, birds."

"Feathers, flowers, wolves, and spiders," added Jack.

"Shadows, light," said Annie.

"Bells, clouds, the moon," said Jack.

"And every time he was unhappy about something, his curiosity seemed to make him happy again," said Annie.

Jack took the angel drawing from Annie and carefully put it back into his pack. "Come on," he said. "We don't want to be late for school." Jack started down the rope ladder, and Annie followed.

Jack and Annie walked together through the sun-bright woods. "I wonder where my new class will be," said Annie.

"Yeah," said Jack, "and I wonder where my desk will be. Close to the window? Or the door?"

"And will Randy and Jenny be in my class again this year?" said Annie.

"Will Joe be in mine?" said Jack.

"Whatever happened to Raymond Johnson?" asked Annie. "Is he coming back this year?"

"I hope so," said Jack. "And who's the new librarian? And the new music teacher?"

"Yeah, and what kind of noses do they have?" said Annie.

Jack laughed. All the questions about school didn't make him nervous anymore. Now he was eager to find out the answers. He quickened his steps. "And how long will it take us to get there, if we walk really, really fast?" he said.

"What if we run?" said Annie.

Jack and Annie started running, as the wind blew through the trees and the leaves fluttered through the air and the birds sang from the branches in the Monday-morning woods.

More About Leonardo da Vinci

Leonardo da Vinci, (say lee-uh-NAR-doh duh VIN-chee) was born on April 15, 1452, in Vinci, Italy, just outside Florence. He died on May 2, 1519, in France.

Leonardo da Vinci lived in a time called the Renaissance (say REN-uh-sahns). *Renaissance* means "rebirth." The time was given this name because in those years, learning and creativity reached new heights after a long period called the Middle Ages. The Renaissance began in Italy in the 1300s and then spread to other parts of

Europe. Leonardo has always been the perfect example of the "Renaissance man," which is a person who has many different talents. He was not only one of the world's greatest painters, but he was also an inventor, mathematician, botanist, geologist, cook, musician, philosopher, engineer, and sculptor.

Monday with a Mad Genius was inspired by many true facts about Leonardo da Vinci, such as his reverse handwriting and his keeping of many notebooks. Historians think that his notebooks may have totaled as many as 13,000 pages, but only 7,000 pages of his writings and drawings have been found.

Leonardo really did begin painting a fresco of a vivid battle scene called *The Battle of Anghiari* in the hall of the great council in Florence. A *fresco* is a plaster painting on a wall or ceiling. *The Battle of Anghiari* was indeed damaged because Leonardo experimented with a new painting technique and parts of the painting melted down the wall. Sadly, he never finished it.

Leonardo really had a great interest in birds and flying. He wrote in one of his notebooks that a bird had visited him as a baby in his cradle. One of his earliest biographers wrote that Leonardo bought caged birds in the market and freed them. Leonardo's notebooks had designs for a flying machine with flapping wings, which he called a "great bird." Leonardo wrote that the "great bird" was about to take its first flight and would fill the universe with amazement and bring "eternal glory to the nest where it was born." It was not recorded that his machine ever flew successfully. It is possible that he or an assistant may have tried to fly the plane and failed.

Leonardo really did take three or four years to paint one of the world's most famous works of art, the *Mona Lisa*. And he really did keep the painting with him until he died. But no one knows—or will ever know—the real reason for the Mona Lisa's mysterious smile.

Turn the page for great activities!

Fun Activities for Jack and Annie and *You*!

Make Your Own Flying Machine!

Leonardo da Vinci had lots of ideas for flying machines. Since there were no engines in his time, people would have supplied all the power if they had tried out any of Leonardo's designs.

There are lots of ways to make your own people-powered flying machines—out of paper! Here are instructions for one of the simplest kinds. There are also lots of Web sites with directions for making more complicated paper planes. Check out www.paperairplanes.co.uk and www.amazingpaperairplanes.com for more ideas.

The Great Bird
You will need:
- one standard 8-1/2 x 11-inch sheet of paper

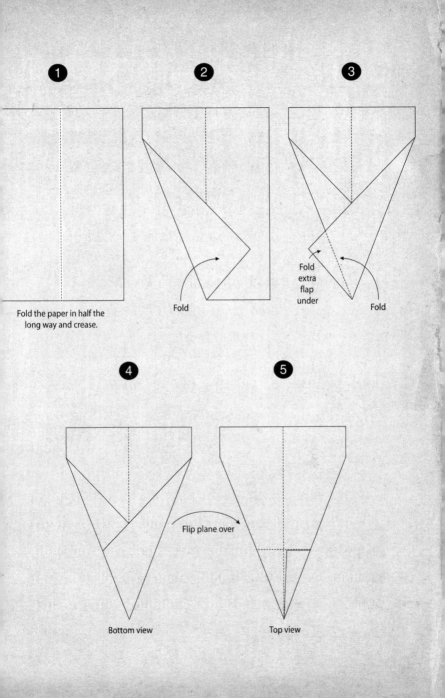

1

Fold the paper in half the long way and crease.

2

Fold

3

Fold
extra
flap
under

Fold

4

Bottom view

5

Flip plane over

Top view

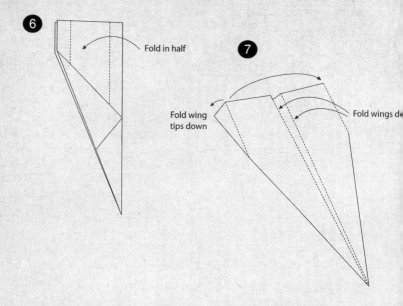

6 Fold in half

7 Fold wing tips down — Fold wings d◀

Hold the center of the plane, then throw it! Have fun!

Puzzle of the Mad Genius

Jack and Annie learned many new things on their adventure with Leonardo da Vinci. Did you?

Put your knowledge to the test with this puzzle. You can use a notebook or make a copy of this page if you don't want to write in your book.

1. The country where Leonardo lives.

☐ ☐ ☐ ☐ ◯

2. A famous painting of a woman with a mysterious smile.

☐ ◯ ☐ ☐

☐ ☐ ☐ ☐

3. The city Leonardo lives in at the time Jack and Annie visit.

☐ ☐ ☐ ☐ ☐ ☐ ◯ ☐

4. Leonardo and Jack both write down their ideas in this.

☐ ☐ ◯ ☐ ☐ ☐ ☐ ☐

5. A brilliant, inventive person.

☐ ☐ ☐ ☐ ◯ ☐

6. Leonardo's name for his flying machine.

☐ ☐ ☐ ☐ ☐

☐ ◯ ☐ ☐

7. To test out new ideas or new ways of doing things.

☐ ☐ ☐ ☐ ☐ ◯ ☐ ☐ ☐ ☐

8. A student who helps and learns from a master artist or master tradesman.

□ □ □ ○ □ □ □ □ □ □

9. A work of art painted over plaster on a wall.

□ □ □ ○ □ □

Now look at your answers above. The letters that are circled spell a word—but that word is scrambled! Can you unscramble it to spell a word that is one of Leonardo's driving forces?

Here's a special preview of
Magic Tree House #39
(A Merlin Mission)
Dark Day in the Deep Sea

Jack and Annie's quest for the secrets
of happiness leads them straight
into the arms of a sea monster.
And it has *a lot* of arms!

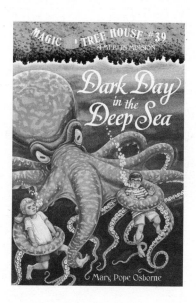

CHAPTER ONE

Back to the Sea

Jack felt raindrops. He looked up and saw a summer storm cloud.

"Hurry!" Jack called to Annie. They were riding their bikes home from the library. Jack's backpack was filled with library books. He didn't want them to get wet.

As Jack and Annie pedaled faster, a large white bird swooped over them and flew into the Frog Creek woods.

"Did you see that?" cried Jack.

"A seagull!" called Annie. "It's a sign!"

"You're right!" said Jack. The last time they'd seen a seagull in Frog Creek, the magic tree house was waiting for them!

"The woods!" said Annie.

Jack and Annie bumped their bikes over the curb. The rain fell harder as they headed into the wet woods. Their bike tires bounced over the rough ground, crushing leaves and snapping twigs.

"It must be time to look for another secret of happiness for Merlin!" Jack called.

"I hope Merlin's feeling better!" shouted Annie.

"I hope Teddy and Kathleen came with the tree house!" shouted Jack.

"Me too!" shouted Annie.

Jack and Annie steered their bikes under canopies of wet leaves. By the time they came to the tallest oak in the woods, the seagull had disappeared. But the magic tree house was back! It was high in the tallest oak, its rope ladder swaying in the wind and rain.

Jack and Annie climbed off their bikes and propped them against the trunk of the tree.

"Teddy! Kathleen!" Annie shouted.

There was no answer.

"I guess they didn't come this time," Jack said.

"Darn!" said Annie. "I really wanted to see them."

"Boo!" Two older kids looked down out of the tree house window: a curly-haired boy with a big grin and a girl with sea-blue eyes and a beautiful smile. Both were wearing long green cloaks.

"Yay!" cried Annie and Jack.

The rain fell harder as they started up the rope ladder. When they climbed into the tree house, they yanked off their bike helmets and hugged Teddy and Kathleen.

"Morgan sent us to tell you about your next mission for Merlin," said Teddy.

"How *is* Merlin?" asked Annie.

Teddy stopped smiling. He shook his head.

"Merlin still suffers from an unspoken sorrow," Kathleen said sadly.

"When can we see him?" asked Annie.

"We've learned two secrets of happiness to share with him," said Jack.

"You may visit him after you have learned two more secrets," said Kathleen. "Morgan believes four is the magic number that will ensure success."

"We have come to send you on your search for a third secret," said Teddy.

Kathleen took a book from under her cloak and handed it to Jack and Annie. "From Morgan's hands to our hands to yours," she said.

Jack took the book from her. The cover showed waves crashing on a beach.

"Wow," said Jack. "We're going to the ocean?"

"Yes," said Teddy. "That is where you will next search for a secret of happiness."

"The ocean always makes me happy," said Annie. "Once Jack and I traveled to a coral reef and swam with dolphins. And we ran into an octopus. But he was nice and shy and—"

"But the shark we saw *wasn't* shy," Jack broke in. "It was a big hammerhead."

"Oh, my," said Kathleen.

"We took a ride in a mini-sub," said Annie. "It was so cool!"

"Until it started to leak and—" said Jack.

"We had to escape!" said Annie.

"Yeah," said Jack. "We tried not to splash—so the shark wouldn't notice us."

"We had so much fun!" said Annie.

Kathleen smiled. "Well, I hope you will not find the same 'fun' on this journey," she said.

"But in case you do, you have your wand to help you, do you not?" asked Teddy. "The Wand of Dianthus?"

"Of course," said Jack. "I always carry it, just in case." Jack reached into his backpack and pulled out the silvery wand. It was shaped like the spiraled horn of a unicorn.

"You remember the three rules?" asked Kathleen.

"Sure," said Jack. "To make magic, we use a wish with only five words."

"And before we use the wand, we have to try our hardest," said Annie.

"And the wand can only be used for the good of others," said Jack, "not just ourselves."

"Exactly," said Teddy.

"I wonder who the 'others' will be on this mission," said Annie. She looked at Teddy and Kathleen. "Maybe you guys?"

"I fear not," said Kathleen. "You must find the third secret on your own."

"Just remember to keep your wits about you," said Teddy.

"And listen to your hearts," said Kathleen.

"Okay," said Annie. "We'll tell you all about it when we see you again."

Lightning flashed through the woods as Jack pointed to the cover of the ocean book. "I wish we could go there!" he said.

Thunder cracked in the dark sky. The wind blew harder.

The tree house started to spin.

It spun faster and faster.

Then everything was still.

Absolutely still.

Discover the facts
behind the fiction with the

MAGIC TREE HOUSE®
RESEARCH GUIDES

The must-have, all-true companions for your
favorite Magic Tree House® adventures!

Mary Pope Osborne

is the author of many novels, story collections, and nonfiction books. Her bestselling Magic Tree House series has been translated into numerous languages around the world. Highly recommended by parents and educators everywhere (and kid-approved!), the series introduces young readers to different cultures and times in history, as well as to the world's legacy of ancient myth and storytelling. She and her husband, writer Will Osborne, live in northwestern Connecticut with their two dogs, Joey and Mr. Bezo. The Osbornes invite you to visit their Web sites: www.marypopeosborne.com and www.MTHmusical.com.

Sal Murdocca is best known for his amazing work on the Magic Tree House series. He has written and/or illustrated over two hundred children's books, including *Dancing Granny* by Elizabeth Winthrop, *Double Trouble in Walla Walla* by Andrew Clements, and *Big Numbers* by Edward Packard. He has taught writing and illustration at the Parsons School of Design in New York. He is the librettist for a children's opera and has recently completed his second short film. Sal Murdocca is an avid runner, hiker, and bicyclist. He has often bicycle-toured in Europe and has had many one-man shows of his paintings from these trips. He lives and works with his wife, Nancy, in New City, New York.